'A ghastly
groan and
a shudder. . .'

SHERIDAN LE FANU
Born 1814, Dublin, Ireland
Died 1873, Dublin, Ireland

'Green Tea' was first published in 1872.

LE FANU IN PENGUIN CLASSICS
The Penguin Book of Ghost Stories
Uncle Silas

SHERIDAN LE FANU

Green Tea

PENGUIN BOOKS

PENGUIN CLASSICS

UK | USA | Canada | Ireland | Australia
India | New Zealand | South Africa

Penguin Classics is part of the Penguin Random House group of companies
whose addresses can be found at global.penguinrandomhouse.com.

This edition first published in Penguin Classics in 2016
001

Set in 9/12.4 pt Baskerville 10 Pro
Typeset by Jouve (UK), Milton Keynes
Printed in Great Britain by Clays Ltd, St Ives plc

A CIP catalogue record for this book is available from the British Library

ISBN: 978–0–241–25164–5

Prologue

Though carefully educated in medicine and surgery, I have never practised either. The study of each continues, nevertheless, to interest me profoundly. Neither idleness nor caprice caused my secession from the honourable calling which I had just entered. The cause was a very trifling scratch inflicted by a dissecting knife. This trifle cost me the loss of two fingers, amputated promptly, and the more painful loss of my health, for I have never been quite well since, and have seldom been twelve months together in the same place.

In my wanderings I became acquainted with Dr Martin Hesselius, a wanderer like myself, like me a physician, and like me an enthusiast in his profession. Unlike me in this, that his wanderings were voluntary, and he a man, if not of fortune, as we estimate fortune in England, at least in what our forefathers used to term 'easy circumstances.' He was an old man when I first saw him; nearly five-and-thirty years my senior.

In Dr Martin Hesselius, I found my master. His knowledge was immense, his grasp of a case was an intuition. He was the very man to inspire a young enthusiast, like me, with awe and delight. My admiration has stood the test of

1

time and survived the separation of death. I am sure it was well-founded.

For nearly twenty years I acted as his medical secretary. His immense collection of papers he has left in my care, to be arranged, indexed and bound. His treatment of some of these cases is curious. He writes in two distinct characters. He describes what he saw and heard as an intelligent layman might, and when in this style of narrative he had seen the patient either through his own hall-door, to the light of day, or through the gates of darkness to the caverns of the dead, he returns upon the narrative, and in the terms of his art, and with all the force and originality of genius, proceeds to the work of analysis, diagnosis and illustration.

Here and there a case strikes me as of a kind to amuse or horrify a lay reader with an interest quite different from the peculiar one which it may possess for an expert. With slight modifications, chiefly of language, and of course a change of names, I copy the following. The narrator is Dr Martin Hesselius. I find it among the voluminous notes of cases which he made during a tour in England about sixty-four years ago.

It is related in a series of letters to his friend Professor Van Loo of Leyden. The professor was not a physician, but a chemist, and a man who read history and metaphysics and medicine, and had, in his day, written a play.

The narrative is therefore, if somewhat less valuable as a medical record, necessarily written in a manner more likely to interest an unlearned reader.

These letters, from a memorandum attached, appear to have been returned on the death of the professor, in 1819, to

Dr Hesselius. They are written, some in English, some in French, but the greater part in German. I am a faithful, though I am conscious, by no means a graceful translator, and although here and there, I omit some passages, and shorten others and disguise names, I have interpolated nothing.

Chapter I

DR HESSELIUS RELATES HOW HE MET THE REV. MR JENNINGS

The Rev. Mr Jennings is tall and thin. He is middle-aged, and dresses with a natty, old-fashioned, high-church precision. He is naturally a little stately, but not at all stiff. His features, without being handsome, are well formed, and their expression extremely kind, but also shy.

I met him one evening at Lady Mary Heyduke's. The modesty and benevolence of his countenance are extremely prepossessing.

We were but a small party, and he joined agreeably enough in the conversation. He seems to enjoy listening very much more than contributing to the talk; but what he says is always to the purpose and well said. He is a great favourite of Lady Mary's, who it seems, consults him upon many things, and thinks him the most happy and blessed person on earth. Little knows she about him.

The Rev. Mr Jennings is a bachelor, and has, they say, sixty thousand pounds in the funds. He is a charitable man. He is most anxious to be actively employed in his sacred profession, and yet though always tolerably well elsewhere, when he goes down to his vicarage in Warwickshire, to engage in the actual duties of his sacred calling his health soon fails him, and in a very strange way. So says Lady Mary.

There is no doubt that Mr Jennings' health does break down in, generally a sudden and mysterious way, sometimes in the very act of officiating in his old and pretty church at Kenlis. It may be his heart, it may be his brain. But so it has happened three or four times, or oftener, that after proceeding a certain way in the service, he has on a sudden stopped short, and after a silence, apparently quite unable to resume, he has fallen into solitary, inaudible prayer, his hands and eyes uplifted, and then pale as death, and in the agitation of a strange shame and horror, descended trembling, and got into the vestry-room, leaving his congregation, without explanation, to themselves. This occurred when his curate was absent. When he goes down to Kenlis, now, he always takes care to provide a clergyman to share his duty, and to supply his place on the instant should he become thus suddenly incapacitated.

When Mr Jennings breaks down quite, and beats a retreat from the vicarage, and returns to London, where, in a dark street off Piccadilly, he inhabits a very narrow house, Lady Mary says that he is always perfectly well. I have my own opinion about that. There are degrees of course. We shall see.

Mr Jennings is a perfectly gentleman-like man. People, however, remark something odd. There is an impression a little ambiguous. One thing which certainly contributes to it, people I think don't remember; or, perhaps, distinctly remark. But I did, almost immediately. Mr Jennings has a way of looking sidelong upon the carpet, as if his eye followed the movements of something there. This, of course, is not always. It occurs only now and then. But often enough to give a certain oddity, as I have said to his manner, and in this glance travelling along the floor there is something both shy and anxious.

A medical philosopher, as you are good enough to call me, elaborating theories by the aid of cases sought out by himself, and by him watched and scrutinized with more time at command, and consequently infinitely more minuteness than the ordinary practitioner can afford, falls insensibly into habits of observation, which accompany him everywhere, and are exercised, as some people would say, impertinently, upon every subject that presents itself with the least likelihood of rewarding inquiry.

There was a promise of this kind in the slight, timid, kindly, but reserved gentleman, whom I met for the first time at this agreeable little evening gathering. I observed, of course, more than I here set down; but I reserve all that borders on the technical for a strictly scientific paper.

I may remark, that when I here speak of medical science, I do so, as I hope some day to see it more generally understood, in a much more comprehensive sense than its generally material treatment would warrant. I believe the entire natural world is but the ultimate expression of that spiritual world from which, and in which alone, it has its life. I believe that the essential man is a spirit, that the spirit is an organized substance, but as different in point of material from what we ordinarily understand by matter, as light or electricity is; that the material body is, in the most literal sense, a vesture, and death consequently no interruption of the living man's existence, but simply his extrication from the natural body – a process which commences at the moment of what we term death, and the completion of which, at furthest a few days later, is the resurrection 'in power.'

The person who weighs the consequences of these positions will probably see their practical bearing upon medical science. This is, however, by no means the proper place for displaying the proofs and discussing the consequences of this too generally unrecognized state of facts.

In pursuance of my habit, I was covertly observing Mr Jennings, with all my caution – I think he perceived it – and I saw plainly that he was as cautiously observing me. Lady Mary happening to address me by my name, as Dr Hesselius, I saw that he glanced at me more sharply, and then became thoughtful for a few minutes.

After this, as I conversed with a gentleman at the other end of the room, I saw him look at me more steadily, and with an interest which I thought I understood. I then saw him take an opportunity of chatting with Lady Mary, and was, as one always is, perfectly aware of being the subject of a distant inquiry and answer.

This tall clergyman approached me by-and-by: and in a little time we had got into conversation. When two people, who like reading, and know books and places, having travelled, wish to converse, it is very strange if they can't find topics. It was not accident that brought him near me, and led him into conversation. He knew German, and had read my Essays on Metaphysical Medicine which suggest more than they actually say.

This courteous man, gentle, shy, plainly a man of thought and reading, who moving and talking among us, was not altogether of us, and whom I already suspected of leading a life whose transactions and alarms were carefully concealed, with an impenetrable reserve from, not only the world, but his best beloved friends – was cautiously weighing in his own mind the idea of taking a certain step with regard to me.

I penetrated his thoughts without his being aware of it, and was careful to say nothing which could betray to his sensitive vigilance my suspicions respecting his position, or my surmises about his plans respecting myself.

We chatted upon indifferent subjects for a time; but at last he said:

'I was very much interested by some papers of yours, Dr Hesselius, upon what you term Metaphysical Medicine – I read them in German, ten or twelve years ago – have they been translated?'

'No, I'm sure they have not – I should have heard. They would have asked my leave, I think.'

'I asked the publishers here, a few months ago, to get the book for me in the original German; but they tell me it is out of print.'

'So it is, and has been for some years; but it flatters me as an author to find that you have not forgotten my little book, although,' I added, laughing, 'ten or twelve years is a considerable time to have managed without it; but I suppose you have been turning the subject over again in your mind, or something has happened lately to revive your interest in it.'

At this remark, accompanied by a glance of inquiry, a sudden embarrassment disturbed Mr Jennings, analogous to that which makes a young lady blush and look foolish. He dropped his eyes, and folded his hands together uneasily, and looked oddly, and you would have said, guiltily for a moment.

I helped him out of his awkwardness in the best way, by appearing not to observe it, and going straight on, I said: 'Those revivals of interest in a subject happen to me often; one book suggests another, and often sends me back on a wild-goose chase over an interval of twenty years. But if you still care to possess a copy, I shall be only too happy to provide you; I have still got two or three by me – and if you allow me to present one I shall be very much honoured.'

'You are very good indeed,' he said, quite at his ease again, in a moment: 'I almost despaired – I don't know how to thank you.'

'Pray don't say a word; the thing is really so little worth that I am only ashamed of having offered it, and if you thank me any more I shall throw it into the fire in a fit of modesty.'

Mr Jennings laughed. He inquired where I was staying in London, and after a little more conversation on a variety of subjects, he took his departure.

Chapter II

THE DOCTOR QUESTIONS
LADY MARY, AND SHE ANSWERS

'I like your vicar so much, Lady Mary,' said I, so soon as he was gone. 'He has read, travelled, and thought, and having also suffered, he ought to be an accomplished companion.'

'So he is, and, better still, he is a really good man,' said she. 'His advice is invaluable about my schools, and all my little undertakings at Dawlbridge, and he's so painstaking, he takes so much trouble – you have no idea – wherever he thinks he can be of use: he's so good-natured and so sensible.'

'It is pleasant to hear so good an account of his neighbourly virtues. I can only testify to his being an agreeable and gentle companion, and in addition to what you have told me, I think I can tell you two or three things about him,' said I.

'Really!'

'Yes, to begin with, he's unmarried.'

'Yes, that's right, – go on.'

'He has been writing, that is he *was*, but for two or three years perhaps, he has not gone on with his work, and the book was upon some rather abstract subject – perhaps theology.'

'Well, he was writing a book, as you say; I'm not quite sure what it was about, but only that it was nothing that I cared for, very likely you are right, and he certainly did stop – yes.'

'And although he only drank a little coffee here to-night, he likes tea, at least, did like it, extravagantly.'

'Yes, that's *quite* true.'

'He drank green tea, a good deal, didn't he?' I pursued.

'Well, that's very odd! Green tea was a subject on which we used almost to quarrel.'

'But he has quite given that up,' said I.

'So he has.'

'And, now, one more fact. His mother or his father, did you know them?'

'Yes, both; his father is only ten years dead, and their place is near Dawlbridge. We knew them very well,' she answered.

'Well, either his mother or his father – I should rather think his father, saw a ghost,' said I.

'Well, you really are a conjurer, Dr Hesselius.'

'Conjurer or no, haven't I said right?' I answered merrily.

'You certainly have, and it *was* his father: he was a silent, whimsical man, and he used to bore my father about his dreams, and at last he told him a story about a ghost he had seen and talked with, and a very odd story it was. I remember it particularly, because I was so afraid of him. This story was long before he died – when I was quite a child – and his ways were so silent and moping, and he used to drop in, sometimes, in the dusk, when I was alone in the drawing-room, and I used to fancy there were ghosts about him.'

I smiled and nodded.

'And now having established my character as a conjurer I think I must say good-night,' said I.

'But how *did* you find it out?'

'By the planets of course, as the gipsies do,' I answered, and so, gaily, we said good-night.

Next morning I sent the little book he had been inquiring after, and a note to Mr Jennings, and on returning late that evening, I found that he had called, at my lodgings, and left his card. He asked whether I was at home, and asked at what hour he would be most likely to find me.

Does he intend opening his case, and consulting me 'professionally,' as they say? I hope so. I have already conceived a theory about him. It is supported by Lady Mary's answers to my parting questions. I should like much to ascertain from his own lips. But what can I do consistently with good breeding to invite a confession? Nothing. I rather think he meditates one. At all events, my dear Van L., I shan't make myself difficult of access; I mean to return his visit to-morrow. It will be only civil in return for his politeness, to ask to see him. Perhaps something may come of it. Whether much, little, or nothing, my dear Van L., you shall hear.

Chapter III

DR HESSELIUS PICKS UP
SOMETHING IN LATIN BOOKS

Well, I have called at Blank-street.

On inquiring at the door, the servant told me that Mr Jennings was engaged very particularly with a gentleman, a clergyman from Kenlis, his parish in the country. Intending to reserve my privilege and to call again, I merely intimated that I should try another time, and had turned to go, when the servant begged my pardon, and asked me, looking at me a little more attentively than well-bred persons of his order usually do, whether I was Dr Hesselius; and, on learning that I was, he said, 'Perhaps then, sir, you would allow me to mention it to Mr Jennings, for I am sure he wishes to see you.'

The servant returned in a moment, with a message from Mr Jennings, asking me to go into his study, which was in effect his back drawing-room, promising to be with me in a very few minutes.

This was really a study – almost a library. The room was lofty, with two tall slender windows, and rich dark curtains. It was much larger than I had expected, and stored with books on every side, from the floor to the ceiling. The upper carpet – for to my tread it felt that there were two or

14

three – was a Turkey carpet. My steps fell noiselessly. The book-cases standing out, placed the windows, particularly narrow ones, in deep recesses. The effect of the room was, although extremely comfortable, and even luxurious, decidedly gloomy, and aided by the silence, almost oppressive. Perhaps, however, I ought to have allowed something for association. My mind had connected peculiar ideas with Mr Jennings. I stepped into this perfectly silent room, of a very silent house, with a peculiar foreboding; and its darkness, and solemn clothing of books, for except where two narrow looking-glasses were set in the wall, they were everywhere, helped this sombre feeling.

While awaiting Mr Jennings' arrival, I amused myself by looking into some of the books with which his shelves were laden. Not among these, but immediately under them, with their backs upward, on the floor, I lighted upon a complete set of Swedenborg's Arcana Cælestia, in the original Latin, a very fine folio set, bound in the natty livery which theology affects, pure vellum, namely, gold letters, and carmine edges. There were paper markers in several of these volumes, I raised and placed them, one after the other, upon the table, and opening where these papers were placed, I read in the solemn Latin phraseology, a series of sentences indicated by a pencilled line at the margin. Of these I copy here a few, translating them into English.

'When man's interior sight is opened, which is that of his spirit, then there appear the things of another life, which cannot possibly be made visible to the bodily sight.' . . .

'By the internal sight it has been granted me to see the things that are in the other life, more clearly than I see those that are in the world. From these considerations, it is evident that external vision exists from interior vision, and this from a vision still more interior, and so on.' . . .

'There are with every man at least two evil spirits.' . . .

'With wicked genii there is also a fluent speech, but harsh and grating. There is also among them a speech which is not fluent, wherein the dissent of the thoughts is perceived as something secretly creeping along within it.' . . .

'The evil spirits associated with man are, indeed, from the hells, but when with man they are not then in hell, but are taken out thence. The place where they then are is in the midst between heaven and hell, and is called the world of spirits – when the evil spirits who are with man, are in that world, they are not in any infernal torment, but in every thought and affection of the man, and so, in all that the man himself enjoys. But when they are remitted into their hell, they return to their former state.' . . .

'If evil spirits could perceive that they were associated with man, and yet that they were spirits separate from him, and if they could flow in into the things of his body, they would attempt by a thousand means to destroy him; for they hate man with a deadly hatred.' . . .

'Knowing, therefore, that I was a man in the body, they were continually striving to destroy me, not as to the body only, but especially as to the soul; for to destroy any man or spirit is the very delight of the life of all who are in hell; but I have been continually protected by the Lord. Hence it appears how dangerous it is for man to be in a living consort with spirits, unless he be in the good of faith.' . . .

'Nothing is more carefully guarded from the knowledge

of associate spirits than their being thus conjoint with a man, for if they knew it they would speak to him, with the intention to destroy him.' . . .

'The delight of hell is to do evil to man, and to hasten his eternal ruin.'

A long note, written with a very sharp and fine pencil, in Mr Jennings' neat hand, at the foot of the page, caught my eye. Expecting his criticism upon the text, I read a word or two, and stopped, for it was something quite different, and began with these words, *Deus misereatur mei* – 'May God compassionate me.' Thus warned of its private nature, I averted my eyes, and shut the book, replacing all the volumes as I had found them, except one which interested me, and in which, as men studious and solitary in their habits will do, I grew so absorbed as to take no cognizance of the outer world, nor to remember where I was.

I was reading some pages which refer to 'representatives' and 'correspondents,' in the technical language of Swedenborg, and had arrived at a passage, the substance of which is, that evil spirits, when seen by other eyes than those of their infernal associates, present themselves, by 'correspondence,' in the shape of the beast (*fera*) which represents their particular lust and life, in aspect direful and atrocious. This is a long passage, and particularizes a number of those bestial forms.

Chapter IV

I was running the head of my pencil-case along the line as I read it, and something caused me to raise my eyes.

Directly before me was one of the mirrors I have mentioned, in which I saw reflected the tall shape of my friend Mr Jennings leaning over my shoulder, and reading the page at which I was busy, and with a face so dark and wild that I should hardly have known him.

I turned and rose. He stood erect also, and with an effort laughed a little, saying:

'I came in and asked you how you did, but without succeeding in awaking you from your book; so I could not restrain my curiosity, and very impertinently, I'm afraid, peeped over your shoulder. This is not your first time of looking into those pages. You have looked into Swedenborg, no doubt, long ago?'

'Oh dear, yes! I owe Swedenborg a great deal; you will discover traces of him in the little book on Metaphysical Medicine, which you were so good as to remember.'

Although my friend affected a gaiety of manner, there was a slight flush in his face, and I could perceive that he was inwardly much perturbed.

'I'm scarcely yet qualified, I know so little of Swedenborg.

I've only had them a fortnight,' he answered, 'and I think they are rather likely to make a solitary man nervous – that is, judging from the very little I have read – I don't say that they have made me so,' he laughed; 'and I'm so very much obliged for the book. I hope you got my note?'

I made all proper acknowledgments and modest disclaimers.

'I never read a book that I go with, so entirely, as that of yours,' he continued. 'I saw at once there is more in it than is quite unfolded. Do you know Dr Harley?' he asked, rather abruptly.

In passing, the editor remarks that the physician here named was one of the most eminent who had ever practised in England.

I did, having had letters to him, and had experienced from him great courtesy and considerable assistance during my visit to England.

'I think that man one of the very greatest fools I ever met in my life,' said Mr Jennings.

This was the first time I had ever heard him say a sharp thing of anybody, and such a term applied to so high a name a little startled me.

'Really! and in what way?' I asked.

'In his profession,' he answered.

I smiled.

'I mean this,' he said: 'he seems to me, one half, blind – I mean one half of all he looks at is dark – preternaturally bright and vivid all the rest; and the worst of it is, it seems *wilful*. I can't get him – I mean he won't – I've had some experience of him as a physician, but I look on him as, in

19

that sense, no better than a paralytic mind, an intellect half dead, I'll tell you – I know I shall some time – all about it,' he said, with a little agitation. 'You stay some months longer in England. If I should be out of town during your stay for a little time, would you allow me to trouble you with a letter?'

'I should be only too happy,' I assured him.

'Very good of you. I am so utterly dissatisfied with Harley.'

'A little leaning to the materialistic school,' I said.

'A *mere* materialist,' he corrected me; 'you can't think how that sort of thing worries one who knows better. You won't tell any one – any of my friends you know – that I am hippish; now, for instance, no one knows – not even Lady Mary – that I have seen Dr Harley, or any other doctor. So pray don't mention it; and, if I should have any threatening of an attack, you'll kindly let me write, or, should I be in town, have a little talk with you.'

I was full of conjecture, and unconsciously I found I had fixed my eyes gravely on him, for he lowered his for a moment, and he said:

'I see you think I might as well tell you now, or else you are forming a conjecture; but you may as well give it up. If you were guessing all the rest of your life, you will never hit on it.'

He shook his head smiling, and over that wintry sunshine a black cloud suddenly came down, and he drew his breath in, through his teeth as men do in pain.

'Sorry, of course, to learn that you apprehend occasion to

consult any of us; but, command me when and how you like, and I need not assure you that your confidence is sacred.'

He then talked of quite other things, and in a comparatively cheerful way and after a little time, I took my leave.

Chapter V

DOCTOR HESSELIUS IS
SUMMONED TO RICHMOND

We parted cheerfully, but he was not cheerful, nor was I. There are certain expressions of that powerful organ of spirit – the human face – which, although I have seen them often, and possess a doctor's nerve, yet disturb me profoundly. One look of Mr Jennings haunted me. It had seized my imagination with so dismal a power that I changed my plans for the evening, and went to the opera, feeling that I wanted a change of ideas.

I heard nothing of or from him for two or three days, when a note in his hand reached me. It was cheerful, and full of hope. He said that he had been for some little time so much better – quite well, in fact – that he was going to make a little experiment, and run down for a month or so to his parish, to try whether a little work might not quite set him up. There was in it a fervent religious expression of gratitude for his restoration, as he now almost hoped he might call it.

A day or two later I saw Lady Mary, who repeated what his note had announced, and told me that he was actually in Warwickshire, having resumed his clerical duties at Kenlis; and she added, 'I begin to think that he is really perfectly well, and that there never was anything the matter, more

than nerves and fancy; we are all nervous, but I fancy there
is nothing like a little hard work for that kind of weakness,
and he has made up his mind to try it. I should not be sur-
prised if he did not come back for a year.'

Notwithstanding all this confidence, only two days later
I had this note, dated from his house off Piccadilly:

Dear Sir. – I have returned disappointed. If I should feel at
all able to see you, I shall write to ask you kindly to call. At
present I am too low, and, in fact, simply unable to say all I
wish to say. Pray don't mention my name to my friends. I can
see no one. By-and-by, please God, you shall hear from me. I
mean to take a run into Shropshire, where some of my people
are. God bless you! May we, on my return, meet more happily
than I can now write.

About a week after this I saw Lady Mary at her own house,
the last person, she said, left in town, and just on the wing
for Brighton, for the London season was quite over. She told
me she had heard from Mr Jennings' niece, Martha, in
Shropshire. There was nothing to be gathered from her letter, more than that he was low and nervous. In those words,
of which healthy people think so lightly, what a world of
suffering is sometimes hidden!

Nearly five weeks passed without any further news of Mr
Jennings. At the end of that time I received a note from him.
He wrote:

I have been in the country, and have had change of air,
change of scene, change of faces, change of everything and
in everything – but *myself.* I have made up my mind, so far as

23

the most irresolute creature on earth can do it, to tell my case fully to you. If your engagements will permit, pray come to me to-day, to-morrow, or the next day; but, pray defer as little as possible. You know not how much I need help. I have a quiet house at Richmond, where I now am. Perhaps you can manage to come to dinner, or to luncheon, or even to tea. You shall have no trouble in finding me out. The servant at Blank street, who takes this note, will have a carriage at your door at any hour you please; and I am always to be found. You will say that I ought not to be alone. I have tried everything. Come and see.

I called up the servant, and decided on going out the same evening, which accordingly I did.

He would have been much better in a lodging-house, or hotel, I thought, as I drove up through a short double row of sombre elms to a very old-fashioned brick house, darkened by the foliage of these trees, which over-topped, and nearly surrounded it. It was a perverse choice, for nothing could be imagined more triste and silent. The house, I found, belonged to him. He had stayed for a day or two in town, and, finding it for some cause insupportable, had come out here, probably because being furnished and his own, he was relieved of the thought and delay of selection, by coming here.

The sun had already set, and the red reflected light of the western sky illuminated the scene with the peculiar effect with which we are all familiar. The hall seemed very dark, but, getting to the back drawing-room, whose windows command the west, I was again in the same dusky light.

I sat down, looking out upon the richly-wooded landscape that glowed in the grand and melancholy light which was every moment fading. The corners of the room were already dark; all was growing dim, and the gloom was insensibly toning my mind, already prepared for what was sinister. I was waiting alone for his arrival, which soon took place. The door communicating with the front room opened, and the tall figure of Mr Jennings, faintly seen in the ruddy twilight, came, with quiet stealthy steps, into the room.

We shook hands, and, taking a chair to the window, where there was still light enough to enable us to see each other's faces, he sat down beside me, and, placing his hand upon my arm, with scarcely a word of preface began his narrative.

Chapter VI

HOW MR JENNINGS MET HIS COMPANION

The faint glow of the west, the pomp of the then lonely woods of Richmond, were before us, behind and about us the darkening room, and on the stony face of the sufferer – for the character of his face, though still gentle and sweet, was changed – rested that dim, odd glow which seems to descend and produce, where it touches, lights, sudden though faint, which are lost, almost without gradation, in darkness. The silence, too, was utter; not a distant wheel, or bark, or whistle from without; and within the depressing stillness of an invalid bachelor's house.

I guessed well the nature, though not even vaguely the particulars of the revelations I was about to receive, from that fixed face of suffering that so oddly flushed stood out, like a portrait of Schalken's, before its background of darkness.

'It began,' he said, 'on the 15th of October, three years and eleven weeks ago, and two days – I keep very accurate count, for every day is torment. If I leave anywhere a chasm in my narrative tell me.

'About four years ago I began a work, which had cost me very much thought and reading. It was upon the religious metaphysics of the ancients.'

'I know,' said I; 'the actual religion of educated and thinking paganism, quite apart from symbolic worship? A wide and very interesting field.'

'Yes; but not good for the mind – the Christian mind, I mean. Paganism is all bound together in essential unity, and, with evil sympathy, their religion involves their art, and both their manners, and the subject is a degrading fascination and the nemesis sure. God forgive me!

'I wrote a great deal; I wrote late at night. I was always thinking on the subject, walking about, wherever I was, everywhere. It thoroughly infected me. You are to remember that all the material ideas connected with it were more or less of the beautiful, the subject itself delightfully interesting, and I, then, without a care.'

He sighed heavily.

'I believe that every one who sets about writing in earnest does his work, as a friend of mine phrased it, *on* something – tea, or coffee, or tobacco. I suppose there is a material waste that must be hourly supplied in such occupations, or that we should grow too abstracted, and the mind, as it were, pass out of the body, unless it were reminded often of the connection by actual sensation. At all events, I felt the want, and I supplied it. Tea was my companion – at first the ordinary black tea, made in the usual way, not too strong: but I drank a good deal, and increased its strength as I went on. I never experienced an uncomfortable symptom from it. I began to take a little green tea. I found the effect pleasanter, it cleared and intensified the power of thought so. I had come to take it frequently, but not stronger than one might take it for pleasure. I wrote a great deal out here, it was so quiet, and in this room. I used to sit up very late, and it became a habit with me to sip my tea – green tea – every now and then as my work proceeded. I had a little kettle on my table, that swung over a lamp, and made tea two or three times between eleven o'clock and two or three in the morning, my hours of going to bed. I used to go into town every day. I was not a monk, and, although I spent an hour or two in a library, hunting up authorities and looking out lights upon my theme, I was in no morbid state as far as I can judge. I met my friends pretty much as usual, and enjoyed their society, and, on the whole, existence had never been, I think, so pleasant before.

'I had met with a man who had some odd old books, German editions in mediæval Latin, and I was only too happy to be permitted access to them. This obliging person's books were in the City, a very out-of-the-way part of it. I had rather out-stayed my intended hour, and, on coming out, seeing no cab near, I was tempted to get into the omnibus which used to drive past this house. It was darker than this by the time the 'bus had reached an old house, you may have remarked, with four poplars at each side of the door, and there the last passenger but myself got out. We drove along rather faster. It was twilight now. I leaned back in my corner next the door ruminating pleasantly.

'The interior of the omnibus was nearly dark. I had observed in the corner opposite to me at the other side, and at the end next the horses, two small circular reflections, as it seemed to me of a reddish light. They were about two inches apart, and about the size of those small brass buttons that yachting men used to put upon their jackets. I began to speculate, as listless men will, upon this trifle, as it seemed. From what centre did that faint but deep red light come, and from what – glass beads, buttons, toy decorations – was it reflected? We were lumbering along gently, having nearly a mile still to go. I had not solved the puzzle, and it became in another minute more odd, for these two luminous points, with a sudden jerk, descended nearer the floor, keeping still their relative distance and horizontal position, and then, as suddenly, they rose to the level of the seat on which I was sitting, and I saw them no more.

'My curiosity was now really excited, and, before I had time to think, I saw again these two dull lamps, again together near the floor; again they disappeared, and again in their old corner I saw them.

'So, keeping my eyes upon them, I edged quietly up my own side, towards the end at which I still saw these tiny discs of red.

'There was very little light in the 'bus. It was nearly dark. I leaned forward to aid my endeavour to discover what these little circles really were. They shifted their position a little as I did so. I began now to perceive an outline of something black, and I soon saw with tolerable distinctness the outline of a small black monkey, pushing its face forward in mimicry to meet mine; those were its eyes, and I now dimly saw its teeth grinning at me.

'I drew back, not knowing whether it might not meditate a spring. I fancied that one of the passengers had forgot this ugly pet, and wishing to ascertain something of its temper, though not caring to trust my fingers to it, I poked my umbrella softly towards it. It remained immovable – up to

29

it – *through* it! For through it, and back and forward, it passed, without the slightest resistance.

'I can't, in the least, convey to you the kind of horror that I felt. When I had ascertained that the thing was an illusion, as I then supposed, there came a misgiving about myself and a terror that fascinated me in impotence to remove my gaze from the eyes of the brute for some moments. As I looked, it made a little skip back, quite into the corner, and I, in a panic, found myself at the door, having put my head out, drawing deep breaths of the outer air, and staring at the lights and trees we were passing, too glad to reassure myself of reality.

'I stopped the 'bus and got out. I perceived the man look oddly at me as I paid him. I daresay there was something unusual in my looks and manner, for I had never felt so strangely before.'

Chapter VII

'When the omnibus drove on, and I was alone upon the road, I looked carefully round to ascertain whether the monkey had followed me. To my indescribable relief I saw it nowhere. I can't describe easily what a shock I had received, and my sense of genuine gratitude on finding myself, as I supposed, quite rid of it.

'I had got out a little before we reached this house, two or three hundred steps. A brick wall runs along the footpath, and inside the wall is a hedge of yew or some dark evergreen of that kind, and within that again the row of fine trees which you may have remarked as you came.

'This brick wall is about as high as my shoulder, and happening to raise my eyes I saw the monkey, with that stooping gait, on all fours, walking or creeping, close beside me on top of the wall. I stopped, looking at it with a feeling of loathing and horror. As I stopped so did it. It sat up on the wall with its long hands on its knees looking at me. There was not light enough to see it much more than in outline, nor was it dark enough to bring the peculiar light of its eyes into strong relief. I still saw, however, that red foggy light plainly enough. It did not show its teeth, nor exhibit any

31

sign of irritation, but seemed jaded and sulky, and was observing me steadily.

'I drew back into the middle of the road. It was an unconscious recoil, and there I stood, still looking at it, it did not move.

'With an instinctive determination to try something – anything, I turned about and walked briskly towards town with a skance look, all the time, watching the movements of the beast. It crept swiftly along the wall, at exactly my pace.

'Where the wall ends, near the turn of the road, it came down and with a wiry spring or two brought itself close to my feet, and continued to keep up with me, as I quickened my pace. It was at my left side, so close to my leg that I felt every moment as if I should tread upon it.

'The road was quite deserted and silent, and it was darker every moment. I stopped dismayed and bewildered, turning as I did so, the other way – I mean, towards this house, away from which I had been walking. When I stood still, the monkey drew back to a distance of, I suppose, about five or six yards, and remained stationary, watching me.

'I had been more agitated than I have said. I had read, of course, as every one has, something about "spectral illusions," as you physicians term the phenomena of such cases. I considered my situation, and looked my misfortune in the face.

'These affections, I had read, are sometimes transitory and sometimes obstinate. I had read of cases in which the appearance, at first harmless, had, step by step, degenerated into something direful and insupportable, and ended by wearing its victim out. Still as I stood there, but for my bestial companion, quite alone, I tried to comfort myself by repeating again and again the assurance, "the thing is purely disease, a well-known physical affection, as distinctly as small-pox or neuralgia. Doctors are all agreed on that, philosophy demonstrates it. I must not be a fool. I've been sitting up too late, and I daresay my digestion is quite wrong, and with God's help, I shall be all right, and this is but a symptom of nervous dyspepsia." Did I believe all this? Not one word of it, no more than any other miserable being ever did who is once seized and riveted in this satanic captivity. Against my convictions, I might say my knowledge, I was simply bullying myself into a false courage.

'I now walked homeward. I had only a few hundred yards to go. I had forced myself into a sort of resignation, but I had not got over the sickening shock and the flurry of the first certainty of my misfortune.

'I made up my mind to pass the night at home. The brute moved close beside me, and I fancied there was the sort of anxious drawing toward the house, which one sees in tired horses or dogs, sometimes as they come toward home.

'I was afraid to go into town, I was afraid of any one's seeing and recognizing me. I was conscious of an irrepressible agitation in my manner. Also, I was afraid of any violent change in my habits, such as going to a place of amusement, or walking from home in order to fatigue myself. At the hall door it waited till I mounted the steps, and when the door was opened entered with me.

'I drank no tea that night. I got cigars and some brandy-and-water. My idea was that I should act upon my material system, and by living for a while in sensation apart from thought, send myself forcibly, as it it were, into a new groove. I came up here to this drawing-room. I sat just here. The monkey then got upon a small table that then stood *there*. It looked dazed and languid. An irrepressible uneasiness as to its movements kept my eyes always upon it. Its eyes were half closed, but I could see them glow. It was looking steadily at me. In all situations, at all hours, it is awake and looking at me. That never changes.

'I shall not continue in detail my narrative of this particular night. I shall describe, rather, the phenomena of the first year, which never varied, essentially. I shall describe the monkey as it appeared in daylight. In the dark, as you shall presently hear, there are peculiarities. It is a small monkey, perfectly black. It had only one peculiarity – a character of malignity – unfathomable malignity. During the first year it looked sullen and sick. But this character of intense malice and vigilance was always underlying that surly languor. During all that time it acted as if on a plan of giving me as little trouble as was consistent with watching me. Its eyes were never off me. I have never lost sight of it, except in my sleep, light or dark, day or night, since it came here, excepting when it withdraws for some weeks at a time, unaccountably.

'In total dark it is visible as in daylight. I do not mean merely its eyes. It is *all* visible distinctly in a halo that resembles a glow of red embers, and which accompanies it in all its movements.

'When it leaves me for a time, it is always at night, in the dark, and in the same way. It grows at first uneasy, and then furious, and then advances towards me, grinning and shaking its paws clenched, and, at the same time, there comes the appearance of fire in the grate. I never have any fire. I can't sleep in the room where there is any, and it draws nearer and nearer to the chimney, quivering, it seems, with rage, and when its fury rises to the highest pitch, it springs into the grate, and up the chimney, and I see it no more.

'When first this happened I thought I was released. I was a new man. A day passed – a night – and no return, and a blessed week – a week – another week. I was always on my knees, Dr Hesselius, always, thanking God and praying. A whole month passed of liberty, but on a sudden, it was with me again.'

Chapter VIII

THE SECOND STAGE

'It was with me, and the malice which before was torpid under a sullen exterior, was now active. It was perfectly unchanged in every other respect. This new energy was apparent in its activity and its looks, and soon in other ways.

'For a time, you will understand, the change was shown only in an increased vivacity, and an air of menace, as if it was always brooding over some atrocious plan. Its eyes, as before, were never off me.'

'Is it here now?' I asked.

'No,' he replied, 'it has been absent exactly a fortnight and a day – fifteen days. It has sometimes been away so long as nearly two months, once for three. Its absence always exceeds a fortnight, although it may be but by a single day. Fifteen days having past since I saw it last, it may return now at any moment.'

'Is its return,' I asked, 'accompanied by any peculiar manifestation?'

'Nothing – no,' he said. 'It is simply with me again. On lifting my eyes from a book, or turning my head, I see it, as usual, looking at me, and then it remains, as before, for its appointed time. I have never told so much and so minutely before to any one.'

I perceived that he was agitated, and looking like death, and he repeatedly applied his handkerchief to his forehead; I suggested that he might be tired, and told him that I would call, with pleasure, in the morning, but he said:

'No, if you don't mind hearing it all now. I have got so far, and I should prefer making one effort of it. When I spoke to Dr Harley, I had nothing like so much to tell. You are a philosophic physician. You give spirit its proper rank. If this thing is real –'

He paused, looking at me with agitated inquiry.

'We can discuss it by-and-by, and very fully. I will give you all I think,' I answered, after an interval.

'Well – very well. If it is anything real, I say, it is prevailing, little by little, and drawing me more interiorly into hell. Optic nerves, he talked of. Ah! well – there are other nerves of communication. May God Almighty help me! You shall hear.

'Its power of action, I tell you, had increased. Its malice became, in a way aggressive. About two years ago, some questions that were pending between me and the bishop having been settled, I went down to my parish in Warwickshire, anxious to find occupation in my profession. I was not prepared for what happened, although I have since thought I might have apprehended something like it. The reason of my saying so, is this –'

He was beginning to speak with a great deal more effort and reluctance, and sighed often, and seemed at times nearly overcome. But at this time his manner was not agitated. It was more like that of a sinking patient, who has given himself up.

'Yes, but I will first tell you about Kenlis, my parish.

'It was with me when I left this place for Dawlbridge. It was my silent travelling companion, and it remained with me at the vicarage. When I entered on the discharge of my duties, another change took place. The thing exhibited an atrocious determination to thwart me. It was with me in the church – in the reading-desk – in the pulpit – within the communion rails. At last, it reached this extremity, that while I was reading to the congregation, it would spring upon the open book and squat there, so that I was unable to see the page. This happened more than once.

'I left Dawlbridge for a time. I placed myself in Dr Harley's hands. I did everything he told me. He gave my case a great deal of thought. It interested him, I think. He seemed successful. For nearly three months I was perfectly free from a return. I began to think I was safe. With his full assent I returned to Dawlbridge.

'I travelled in a chaise. I was in good spirits. I was more – I was happy and grateful. I was returning, as I thought delivered from a dreadful hallucination, to the scene of duties which I longed to enter upon. It was a beautiful sunny evening, everything looked serene and cheerful, and I was delighted. I remember looking out of the window to see the spire of my church at Kenlis among the trees, at the point where one has the earliest view of it. It is exactly where the little stream that bounds the parish passes under the road by a culvert, and where it emerges at the road-side, a stone with an old inscription is placed. As we passed this point, I drew my head in and sat down, and in the corner of the chaise was the monkey.

'For a moment I felt faint, and then quite wild with despair and horror. I called to the driver, and got out, and sat down at the road-side, and prayed to God silently for mercy. A despairing resignation supervened. My companion was with me as I re-entered the vicarage. The same persecution followed. After a short struggle I submitted, and soon I left the place.

'I told you,' he said, 'that the beast has before this become in certain ways aggressive. I will explain a little. It seemed to be actuated by intense and increasing fury, whenever I said my prayers, or even meditated prayer. It amounted at last to a dreadful interruption. You will ask, how could a silent immaterial phantom effect that? It was thus, whenever I meditated praying; it was always before me, and nearer and nearer.

'It used to spring on a table, on the back of a chair, on the chimney-piece, and slowly to swing itself from side to side, looking at me all the time. There is in its motion an indefinable power to dissipate thought, and to contract one's attention to that monotony, till the ideas shrink, as it were, to a point, and at last to nothing – and unless I had started up, and shook off the catalepsy I have felt as if my mind were on the point of losing itself. There are other ways,' he sighed heavily; 'thus, for instance, while I pray with my eyes closed, it comes closer and closer, and I see it. I know it is not to be accounted for physically, but I do actually see it, though my lids are closed, and so it rocks my mind, as it were, and overpowers me, and I am obliged to rise from my knees. If you had ever yourself known this, you would be acquainted with desperation.'

Chapter IX

THE THIRD STAGE

'I see, Dr Hesselius, that you don't lose one word of my statement. I need not ask you to listen specially to what I am now going to tell you. They talk of the optic nerves, and of spectral illusions, as if the organ of sight was the only point assailable by the influences that have fastened upon me – I know better. For two years in my direful case that limitation prevailed. But as food is taken in softly at the lips, and then brought under the teeth, as the tip of the little finger caught in a mill crank will draw in the hand, and the arm, and the whole body, so the miserable mortal who has been once caught firmly by the end of the finest fibre of his nerve, is drawn in and in, by the enormous machinery of hell, until he is as I am. Yes, Doctor, as *I* am, for while I talk to you, and implore relief, I feel that my prayer is for the impossible, and my pleading with the inexorable.'

I endeavoured to calm his visibly increasing agitation, and told him that he must not despair.

While we talked the night had overtaken us. The filmy moonlight was wide over the scene which the window commanded, and I said:

'Perhaps you would prefer having candles. This light, you know, is odd. I should wish you, as much as possible, under your usual conditions while I make my diagnosis, shall I call it – otherwise I don't care.'

'All lights are the same to me,' he said: 'except when I read or write, I care not if night were perpetual. I am going to tell you what happened about a year ago. The thing began to speak to me.'

'Speak! How do you mean – speak as a man does, do you mean?'

'Yes; speak in words and consecutive sentences, with perfect coherence and articulation; but there is a peculiarity. It is not like the tone of a human voice. It is not by my ears it reaches me – it comes like a singing through my head.

'This faculty, the power of speaking to me, will be my undoing. It won't let me pray, it interrupts me with dreadful blasphemies. I dare not go on, I could not. Oh! Doctor, can the skill, and thought, and prayers of man avail me nothing!'

'You must promise me, my dear sir, not to trouble yourself with unnecessarily exciting thoughts; confine yourself strictly to the narrative of *facts*; and recollect, above all, that even if the thing that infests you be all you seem to suppose, a reality with an actual independent life and will, yet it can have no power to hurt you, unless it be given from above: its access to your senses depends mainly upon your physical condition – this is, under God, your comfort and reliance: we are all alike environed. It is only that in your case, the "*paries*," the veil of the flesh, the screen, is a little out of repair, and sights and sounds are transmitted. We must enter on a new course, sir – be encouraged. I'll give to-night to the careful consideration of the whole case.'

'You are very good, sir; you think it worth trying, you don't give me quite up; but, sir, you don't know, it is gaining such an influence over me: it orders me about, it is such a tyrant, and I'm growing so helpless. May God deliver me!'

'It orders you about – of course you mean by speech?'

'Yes, yes; it is always urging me to crimes, to injure others, or myself. You see, Doctor, the situation is urgent, it is indeed. When I was in Shropshire, a few weeks ago' (Mr Jennings was speaking rapidly and trembling now, holding my arm with one hand, and looking in my face), 'I went out one day with a party of friends for a walk: my persecutor, I tell you, was with me at the time. I lagged behind the rest: the country near the Dee, you know, is beautiful. Our path happened to lie near a coal mine, and at the verge of the wood is a perpendicular shaft, they say, a hundred and fifty feet deep. My niece had remained behind with me – she knows, of course, nothing of the nature of my sufferings. She knew, however, that I had been ill, and was low, and she remained to prevent my being quite alone. As we loitered slowly on together the brute that accompanied me was urging me to throw myself down the shaft. I tell you now – oh, sir, think of it! – the one consideration that saved me from that hideous death was the fear lest the shock of witnessing the occurrence should be too much for the poor girl. I asked her to go on and take her walk with her friends, saying that I could go no further. She made excuses, and the more I urged her the firmer she became. She looked doubtful and frightened. I suppose there was something in my looks or manner that alarmed her; but she would not go, and that literally saved me. You had no idea, sir, that a living man could be made so abject a slave of Satan,' he said, with a ghastly groan and a shudder.

There was a pause here, and I said, 'You *were* preserved nevertheless. It was the act of God. You are in his hands and in the power of no other being: be therefore confident for the future.'

Chapter X

I made him have candles lighted, and saw the room looking cheery and inhabited before I left him. I told him that he must regard his illness strictly as one dependent on physical, though *subtle* physical, causes. I told him that he had evidence of God's care and love in the deliverance which he had just described, and that I had perceived with pain that he seemed to regard its peculiar features as indicating that he had been delivered over to spiritual reprobation. Than such a conclusion nothing could be, I insisted, less warranted; and not only so, but more contrary to facts, as disclosed in his mysterious deliverance from that murderous influence during his Shropshire excursion. First, his niece had been retained by his side without his intending to keep her near him; and, secondly, there had been infused into his mind an irresistible repugnance to execute the dreadful suggestion in her presence.

As I reasoned this point with him, Mr Jennings wept. He seemed comforted. One promise I exacted, which was that should the monkey at any time return, I should be sent for immediately; and, repeating my assurance that I would give neither time nor thought to any other subject until I had thoroughly investigated his case, and that to-morrow he should hear the result, I took my leave.

Before getting into the carriage I told the servant that his master was far from well, and that he should make a point of frequently looking into his room.

My own arrangements I made with a view to being quite secure from interruption.

I merely called at my lodgings, and with a travelling-desk and carpet-bag, set off in a hackney-carriage for an inn about two miles out of town, called The Horns, a very quiet and comfortable house, with good thick walls. And there I resolved, without the possibility of intrusion or distraction, to devote some hours of the night, in my comfortable sitting-room, to Mr Jennings' case, and so much of the morning as it might require.

(There occurs here a careful note of Dr Hesselius' opinion upon the case and of the habits, dietary, and medicines which he prescribed. It is curious – some persons would say mystical. But on the whole I doubt whether it would sufficiently interest a reader of the kind I am likely to meet with, to warrant its being here reprinted. The whole letter was plainly written at the inn where he had hid himself for the occasion. The next letter is dated from his town lodgings.)

I left town for the inn where I slept last night at half-past nine, and did not arrive at my room in town until one o'clock this afternoon. I found a letter in Mr Jennings' hand upon my table. It had not come by post, and, on inquiry, I learned that Mr Jennings' servant had brought it, and on learning that I was not to return until to-day, and that no one could tell him my address, he seemed very uncomfortable, and said that his orders from his master were that he was not to return without an answer.

I opened the letter, and read:

'Dear Dr Hesselius. It is here. You had not been an hour gone when it returned. It is speaking. It knows all that has happened. It knows everything – it knows you, and is frantic and atrocious. It reviles. I send you this. It knows every word I have written – I write. This I promised, and I therefore write, but I fear very confused, very incoherently. I am so interrupted, disturbed.

'Ever yours, sincerely yours,

'ROBERT LYNDER JENNINGS.'

'When did this come?' I asked.

'About eleven last night: the man was here again, and has been here three times to-day. The last time is about an hour since.'

Thus answered, and with the notes I had made upon his case in my pocket, I was in a few minutes driving towards Richmond, to see Mr Jennings.

I by no means, as you perceive, despaired of Mr Jennings' case. He had himself remembered and applied, though quite in a mistaken way, the principle which I lay down in my Metaphysical Medicine, and which governs all such cases. I was about to apply it in earnest. I was profoundly interested, and very anxious to see and examine him while the 'enemy' was actually present.

I drove up to the sombre house, and ran up the steps, and knocked. The door, in a little time, was opened by a tall woman in black silk. She looked ill, and as if she had been crying. She curtseyed, and heard my question, but she did not answer. She turned her face away, extending her hand towards two men who were coming down-stairs; and thus having, as it were, tacitly made me over to them, she passed through a side-door hastily and shut it.

The man who was nearest the hall, I at once accosted, but being now close to him, I was shocked to see that both his hands were covered with blood.

I drew back a little, and the man passing down-stairs merely said in a low tone, 'Here's the servant, sir.'

The servant had stopped on the stairs, confounded and dumb at seeing me. He was rubbing his hands in a hand-kerchief, and it was steeped in blood.

'Jones, what is it, what has happened?' I asked, while a sickening suspicion overpowered me.

The man asked me to come up to the lobby. I was beside him in a moment, and frowning and pallid, with contracted eyes, he told me the horror which I already half guessed.

His master had made away with himself.

I went upstairs with him to the room – what I saw there I won't tell you. He had cut his throat with his razor. It was a frightful gash. The two men had laid him on the bed and composed his limbs. It had happened, as the immense pool of blood on the floor declared, at some distance between the bed and the window. There was carpet round his bed, and a carpet under his dressing-table, but none on the rest of the floor, for the man said he did not like a carpet on his bedroom. In this sombre, and now terrible room, one of the great elms that darkened the house was slowly moving the shadow of one of its great boughs upon this dreadful floor.

I beckoned to the servant and we went down-stairs together. I turned off the hall into an old-fashioned panelled room, and there standing, I heard all the servant had to tell. It was not a great deal.

'I concluded, sir, from your words, and looks, sir, as you left last night, that you thought my master seriously ill. I thought it might be that you were afraid of a fit, or something. So I attended very close to your directions. He sat up late, till past three o'clock. He was not writing or reading. He was talking a great deal to himself, but that was nothing unusual. At about that hour I assisted him to undress, and left him in his slippers and dressing-gown. I went back softly in about half an hour. He was in his bed, quite undressed, and a pair of candles lighted on the table beside his bed. He was leaning on his elbow and looking out at the other side of the bed when I came in. I asked him if he wanted anything, and he said no.

'I don't know whether it was what you said to me, sir, or something a little unusual about him, but I was uneasy, uncommon uneasy about him last night.

'In another half hour, or it might be a little more, I went up again. I did not hear him talking as before. I opened the door a little. The candles were both out, which was not usual. I had a bedroom candle, and I let the light in, a little bit, looking softly round. I saw him sitting in that chair beside the dressing-table with his clothes on again. He turned round and looked at me. I thought it strange he should get up and dress, and put out the candles to sit in the dark, that way. But I only asked him again if I could do anything for him. He said, no, rather sharp, I thought. I asked if I might light the candles, and he said, "Do as you like, Jones." So I lighted them, and I lingered about the room, and he said, "Tell me truth, Jones, why did you come again – you did not hear any one cursing?" "No, sir," I said, wondering what he could mean.

'"No," said he, after me, "of course, no;" and I said to him, "Wouldn't it be well, sir, you went to bed? It's just five o'clock," and he said nothing but, "Very likely; good-night, Jones." So I went, sir, but in less than an hour I came again. The door was fast, and he heard me, and called as I thought from the bed to know what I wanted, and he desired me not to disturb him again. I lay down and slept for a little. It must have been between six and seven when I went up again. The door was still fast, and he made no answer, so I did not like to disturb him, and thinking he was asleep, I left him till nine. It was his custom to ring when he wished me to come, and I had no particular hour for calling him. I tapped very gently, and getting no answer, I stayed away a good while, supposing he was getting some rest then. It was not till eleven o'clock I grew really uncomfortable about him – for at the latest he was never, that I could remember, later than half-past ten. I got no answer. I knocked and called, and still no answer. So not being able to force the door, I called Thomas from the stables, and together we forced it, and found him in the shocking way you saw.'

Jones had no more to tell. Poor Mr Jennings was very gentle, and very kind. All his people were fond of him. I could see that the servant was very much moved.

So, dejected and agitated, I passed from that terrible house, and its dark canopy of elms, and I hope I shall never see it more. While I write to you I feel like a man who has but half waked from a frightful and monotonous dream.

My memory rejects the picture with incredulity and horror. Yet I know it is true. It is the story of the process of a poison, a poison which excites the reciprocal action of spirit and nerve, and paralyses the tissue that separates those cognate functions of the senses, the external and the interior. Thus we find strange bed-fellows, and the mortal and immortal prematurely make acquaintance.

Conclusion

A WORD FOR THOSE WHO SUFFER

My dear Van L—, you have suffered from an affection similar to that which I have just described. You twice complained of a return of it.

Who, under God, cured you? Your humble servant, Martin Hesselius. Let me rather adopt the more emphasized piety of a certain good old French surgeon of three hundred years ago: 'I treated, and God cured you.'

Come, my friend, you are not to be hippish. Let me tell you a fact.

I have met with, and treated, as my book shows, fifty-seven cases of this kind of vision, which I term indifferently 'sublimated,' 'precocious,' and 'interior.'

There is another class of affections which are truly termed – though commonly confounded with those which I describe – spectral illusions. These latter I look upon as being no less simply curable than a cold in the head or a trifling dyspepsia.

It is those which rank in the first category that test our promptitude of thought. Fifty-seven such cases have I encountered, neither more nor less. And in how many of these have I failed? In no one single instance.

There is no one affliction of mortality more easily and

certainly reducible, with a little patience, and a rational confidence in the physician. With these simple conditions, I look upon the cure as absolutely certain.

You are to remember that I had not even commenced to treat Mr Jennings' case. I have not any doubt that I should have cured him perfectly in eighteen months, or possibly it might have extended to two years. Some cases are very rapidly curable, others extremely tedious. Every intelligent physician who will give thought and diligence to the task, will effect a cure.

You know my tract on The Cardinal Functions of the Brain. I there, by the evidence of innumerable facts, prove, as I think, the high probability of a circulation arterial and venous in its mechanism, through the nerves. Of this system, thus considered, the brain is the heart. The fluid, which is propagated hence through one class of nerves, returns in an altered state through another, and the nature of that fluid is spiritual, though not immaterial, any more than, as I before remarked, light or electricity are so.

By various abuses, among which the habitual use of such agents as green tea is one, this fluid may be affected as to its quality, but it is more frequently disturbed as to equilibrium. This fluid being that which we have in common with spirits, a congestion found upon the masses of brain or nerve, connected with the interior sense, forms a surface unduly exposed, on which disembodied spirits may operate: communication is thus more or less effectually established. Between this brain circulation and the heart circulation there is an intimate sympathy. The seat, or rather the instrument of exterior vision, is the eye. The seat of interior vision is the nervous tissue and brain, immediately about and above the eyebrow. You remember how effectually I dissipated your pictures by the simple application of iced eau-de-cologne. Few cases, however, can be treated exactly alike with anything like rapid success. Cold acts powerfully as a repellant of the nervous fluid. Long enough continued it will even produce that permanent insensibility which we call numbness, and a little longer, muscular as well as sensational paralysis.

I have not, I repeat, the slightest doubt that I should have first dimmed and ultimately sealed that inner eye which Mr Jennings had inadvertently opened. The same senses are opened in delirium tremens, and entirely shut up again when the over-action of the cerebral heart, and the prodigious nervous congestions that attend it, are terminated by a decided change in the state of the body. It is by acting steadily upon the body, by a simple process, that this result is produced – and inevitably produced – I have never yet failed.

Poor Mr Jennings made away with himself. But that catastrophe was the result of a totally different malady, which, as it were, projected itself upon that disease which was established. His case was in the distinctive manner a complication, and the complaint under which he really succumbed, was hereditary suicidal mania. Poor Mr Jennings I cannot call a patient of mine, for I had not even begun to treat his case, and he had not yet given me, I am convinced, his full and unreserved confidence. If the patient do not array himself on the side of the disease, his cure is certain.